ZOLEM

By Brian Bennett

Copyright © 2019 Brian Bennett

All rights reserved.

ISBN: 978-1-6907-2578-7

ZOLEM BY BRIAN BENNETT

Narcoom is a small isolated village in the middle of an uncharted forest, hidden away in the depths of a distant unknown land. When the sun is near, the forest is baking hot, then the days are long and bright, but when the sun is far away and blue, Narcoom is a cold desolate place to live and the days are very short.

The dark forest that surrounds Narcoom provides the villagers with plenty of food but it also has its dangers, from tiny finger nail size spiders that have a red stripe on their backs, to fist sized black hairy eight legged venomous spiders. Add to that the deadly snakes, some only as big as a baby's arm to those that would, given the chance, eat a man whole. Then there is the large lynx-like cat that creeps silently, unseen through the undergrowth and sees man as an easy meal.

On the other hand, there is beauty in the dark forest. Things like the tiny brightly coloured birds that hum as they push their long black tongues deep into the bright exotic flowers in search of the sweet nectar. Their wings moving at such speed that it is impossible to see them, then there are the bigger, rarer birds that are so colourful, that the sun reflects from their blue, green fluorescent red feathers. Also birds that are as big as chickens, that fly screeching through the tree tops, with their long brightly coloured tail feathers that are so rare, they are much desired by the chief and elders of the village.

Monkeys of different sizes leap from tree to tree, screaming at the top of their voices. Violent fights break out amongst the larger males as they challenge for the right to mate with the females.

The constant cacophony of noise slowly dissipates as darkness falls turning the already dark forest pitch black, which is when the screaming giant fruit bats come out. They fly over the village in their thousands, as they make their way to the distant fruit trees. As the day comes to an uneasy end, everything goes quiet unless there is a warning call from the largest male, the king of the monkeys warning the villagers to expect a visit from the dreaded man killing wolf Zolem.

LONG LIVE IGOR

CHAPTER 1

Igor lay trembling in the darkness of his temporary bedroom which he shared with his elderly grandfather. His reed blanket pulled up tight to his chin, not to keep the warmth in, but to keep his fear out. His young heart beat faster than ever. His whole body shook uncontrollably, because he knew that death for both of them was only a few metres away.

The young dark-skinned tribesman strained his ears for the muffled sounds of deep raspy breathing, growling and the inquisitive scratching at the outside wall of his makeshift home. His blue eyes searched the darkness of the barn for any sign of the killer wolf. He knew the threat of death was constant and close. Zolem's putrid pong was everywhere, his signature scent was the only thing that the killer beast left behind, before he returned to his forest lair.

Igor's grandfather, by then a wizened old man needed constant care, simply because he no longer knew who he was or what day of the week it was. Igor had been chosen by his mother to live there to look after his grandfather, as she no longer had the patience or love to look after him, a man who had driven her mad over the last few years, with the slow onset of dementia.

Igor's earliest memory of his grandfather was when he was sat around the camp fire late one summer evening. The old man told the myths and legends handed down from generation to generation. The youngsters of the village, children just like Igor believed every word. Like the story of the Sun God that sent down one single sword of fire, the single flame which created the clearing in the middle of the dark forest, the sacred place in which the villagers have always lived, the secret, mud hut village of Narcoom.

The small, isolated community spoke their own language, had their own laws and beliefs. They had always believed that they had been protected in some way by the closeness and secrecy of the dark forest.

To outsiders, the dense woodland which surrounded it held many hidden dangers, although for the villagers, it had provided all that they had ever needed. The inhabitants were the only ones who knew the few paths, well-worn by hunting parties that were the safe ways in and out.

Because of Zolem, those small, black skinned men, armed only with bows and arrows and poison tipped wooden spears, were the only ones brave enough to hunt for food. Until the wolf appeared they had had nothing to fear.

The large farmhouse named the Nooks, had been built by Igor's missing father. It was the only building in the whole village that had not been built on stilts so that on the strict orders of the wise old chief, if need be, the livestock could be taken in at night, to protect them.

The old leader needed someone that he could trust. He had chosen Igor to fill that most important roll. Igor's new job was to look after, not only his own animals, but also some of the other villager's valuable livestock. The rest of the mud huts were built on long wooden stilts. The only way to access them was by steep narrow ramps which were unsuitable for large animals to walk up. The ramps were made that way, not only to protect the families from the snakes and other deadly animals that hunt by night, but also to keep them safe from the widespread seasonal dangerous floods that were normally a half day walk away.

Heavy monsoon rain sometimes made the muddy waters creep into the village. The deadly waters arrived without warning and stayed for days on end, making hunting and normal village life almost impossible. The wide deep brown water normally provided the villagers with plenty of fish to eat. The long reeds that grew all along the banks of the river were used to create the slanting roofs of the one room huts in which the brightly adorned villagers lived.

In Narcoom, which in the people's ancient language meant "clearing in the wood", each day the tribesmen gathered to worship the rising of the sun and to give thanks for what little they had. The daily ceremony took place just as the sun rose from behind the distant hills. The prayers were held by the chief Axum, a very wise old man, with thick brown leather-like skin. He had dull grey eyes and wore a brightly coloured head dress made out of the tail feathers of the forests many exotic birds. His nose bone was made from part of the head of a big male crocodile. Legend had it that in his younger days he was supposed to have fought and killed the crocodile with his bare hands. The big animal's sharp white teeth, hung proudly around the old man's neck, as a sign of his strength, bravado and virility.

Axum had four wives and many children. He was of a very great age, a very strong, respected leader. But, even with all his wisdom and his lifetime's knowledge of life in the forest, the old chief still had not been able to deal with the deadly threat of Zolem, the large white eyed silver coated male wolf that, one day, had just appeared without warning.

Where the beast came from, no-one knew. Zolem had not only taken most of the village's livestock, but even some of the village residents had, as if by magic, simply disappeared. Those mysterious events nearly always took place in the dead of night. The only way that they knew that the beast had visited at all, was by the obnoxious odour that hung heavily in the air in every section of the village that the wolf had visited.

No matter what precautions the villagers had taken in the past, the ghost-like Zolem always found his mystical way into the village, using his cunning and stealth to search each and every one of the many huts.

The deadly wolf always arrived as if by magic, taking children, dogs, anything that would provide the killer wolf with a meal. Igor had lost almost all of his smaller livestock to the beast, and what few goats and chickens that were left, were kept locked away in the big barn and guarded by Midvant, the biggest, bravest and most dangerous of the horned brown bulls in the village.

Many moons ago in the deepest of the cold white weather, a desperate father and his two sons made their way into the dark forest. They were forced to do this to set traps for food and at the same time collect wood for the fire. When the men had not been heard for two whole days, a search party was sent out to find them. What the searchers eventually discovered was a blood-soaked clearing. The flattened snow had a scattering of torn bloodied clothing and an array of unused, discarded weapons spread all around. There were lots of chewed white bones, legs and arms that had been cleaned of any flesh, shards of jagged edged bones lay everywhere, far too many to collect and take back to the village for burial.

A desperate cry went up from one of the searchers. The other tribesmen rushed to his side, they stood staring at the spot where the killer wolf had lain and eaten his fill of the innocent men. An area as round as a mud hut was stained a bright pink colour, made from the blood of the men. Over to one side, the heads of father and his two sons were found as if laid out as a trophy, the father was missing his right eye. Each of the heads had a swollen black tongue protruding from between their thick black lips.

When Junta lifted the head of his dead friend Kencha, he saw that there was an oval shaped hole the size of a large nut just behind the left ear, the edges of which had been worn smooth by the rough tongue of the killer wolf, as It searched the cavity for the boy's tasty brain. Only the beast, Zolem could be blamed for taking and slaughtering all of the villagers.

On the desperate chief's orders, a hunting party was sent out into the white forest to hunt down and destroy Zolem, but the bitter cold winds and the heavy knee deep snow forced them to return to the village after only one day, because the fresh soft ever deepening white rain had completely covered the deadly killers' tracks.

CHAPTER 2

Terrifying screams filled the darkness of one cold winters night. The terrifying cries for help forced Igor to hide under his cow hide blanket. He cowered with his eyes closed as tightly as he could possibly make them. He began to pray, as his whole body began to shake with uncontrollably fear. His mother, when she last saw him, had scolded him for hiding in his bed at his age and size, when in-fact he should be standing by the barn door, guarding his grandfather against Zolem.

Igor was almost a fully grown man. He was as tall as his wizened old grandfather, a good head taller than his mother and more muscular than any other man in the village. His father had walked into the forest one day long ago in the search of food, and to this day he had never been seen or heard of again.

Axum had said that now it was Igor's turn to be the man of the house, but he was too cowardly. He didn't want the responsibility that the old man had thrust upon him. He didn't know how, nor did he want to be, the head of any household. His mother had said on many occasions that when his grandfather died or was eventually taken by the deadly killer, the whole family would then return to the safety of the farmhouse to live. At that time Igor would then become the man of the house. Then it would be his duty to protect them from the terror of the deadly beast.

The night was bright because of the full moon. The distant star was a big round red ball of light that shone brightly, almost sun-like in the clear star filled sky. The chief held his arms wide and prayed to the Sun God for making the moon shine so bright that some of the older villagers were taking advantage of it and acting as if it was still daytime. The old man thanked the Sun God for sending them so much light that some of the farmers, could continue working the land into the early hours. Igor couldn't sleep and stood by the barn door nervously looking through a small crack.

He watched until very late in the night, when the hairs suddenly stood up on the back of his neck. He was certain that he saw some movement at the edge of the trees, and that could only mean one thing, DANGER!

Igor's heart began to race when he finally saw the beast, Zolem. He watched as the giant wolf continued to walk casually, but at the same time cautiously into the isolated village. The silver coated beast looked magical as the bright moon light reflected from his silver coat, making it luminous, as if a bright star had somehow fallen from the sky, becoming a thing of legend. The huge beast stopped mid stride, raised his black nose and sniffed the night air. He flattened his ears back on his huge head, it was as if he had received some sort of deadly warning. He then turned his evil white eyes towards the barn.

The wolf knew that Igor was watching him. Eventually Zolem seemed to smile at him, taunting and challenging him, before turning and walking silently past into the deathly quiet village. Not long ago there would have been dogs barking a warning of danger, but the beast had taken each and every one of the them. Igor remained where he was listening to the usual night sounds of the forest. He strained his ears for any one sound that was out of place.

The scream that he knew would come, came a short while later. It startled him, instantly making him tremble all over with fear. His teeth were chattering as he stared out into the still bright night. He gasped when he saw the beast come slowly into view.

The monster held a small child grasped in its huge mouth. The young boy was hanging limply in the giant jaws as if he was already dead, but he managed to lift his head, looking pleadingly at the barn door and in a last desperate plea for help, whispered "help me".

It was as if the child could see that Igor was looking at him. Zolem stopped, turned his huge head to look at the barn door. It was as if the devil himself knew that Igor was there. The killer wolf lowered the boys badly wounded body to the ground. The boy began to crawl towards the barn using only his right arm and right leg. His tear filled eyes seemed to be staring straight into Igor's gaze.

Zolem looked down at the boy, turned and ambled towards the barn door, it was as if the beast knew that Igor was there. The wolf turned his head and looked at the boy's useless attempt to escape as he neared the barn door, **"Please save me"** whispered the young lad. The wolf picked the boy up in his huge jaws and looked at the barn door as he nonchalantly crushed the boys tiny rib cage.

The sound of breaking bones and the boy's final moan was all too much for Igor, who closed his eyes as tightly as he could and placed his hands over his ears in a bid to block out the sound of the boy's painful death. Whether it was a warning, a threat, a sign of victory, the wolf walked up to the barn door and pushed one of the boys bloodied arms underneath it.

Igor stepped back and lowered his head in shame. He sank down to his knees and cried. Big fat tears ran freely down his face. He knew then that he was a coward, because he should have gone outside and fought the beast, at least tried to do something, anything, in a bid to save the young boy, even though he knew deep down that he would have most likely been killed himself.

That would have been better than how he felt then. Igor slumped down onto the hard earth floor, not only ashamed, but utterly disgusted with himself.

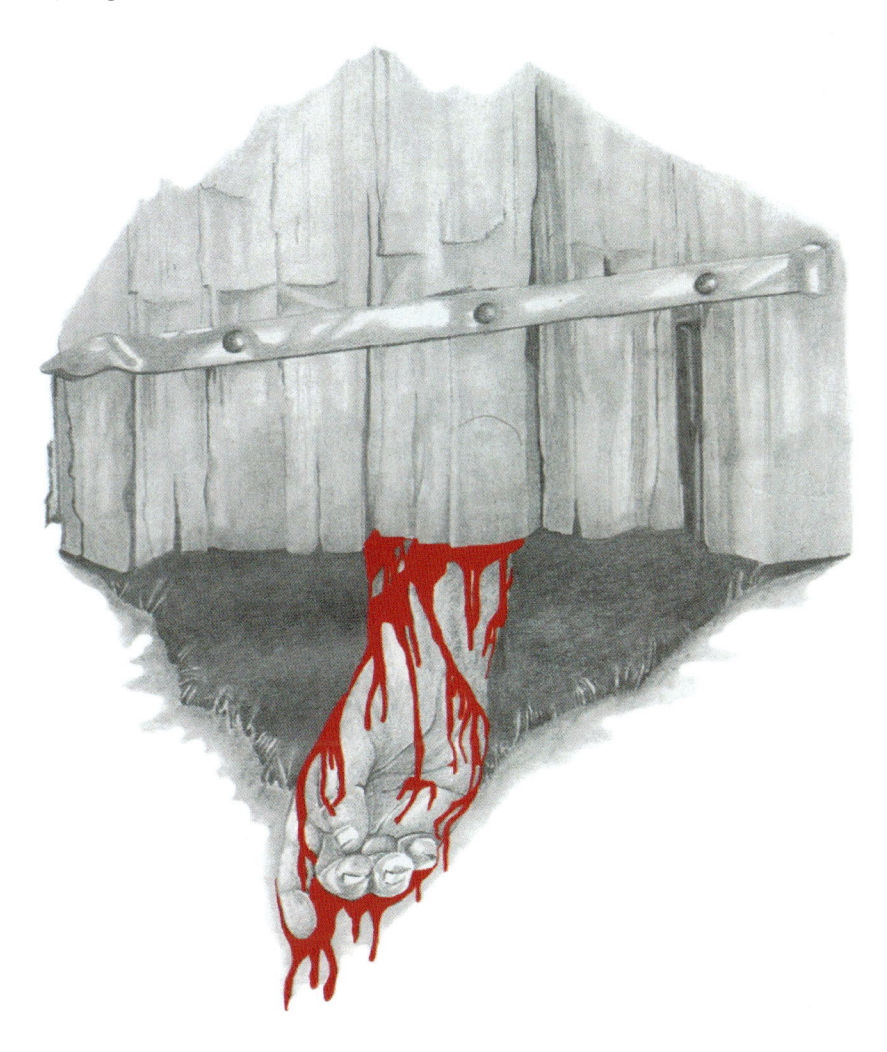

The next morning when he woke, the first vision that came to him was the sight of the now dead boy that had been taken by Zolem, and that arm, he will never forget that small child's bloodied arm. The young innocent lad that had pleaded for his help, and yet he Igor, had done nothing. He would never forget the look in the child's eyes, because the boy knew that he was about to die and then be eaten. In his last moments on this earth the young boy had begged Igor for help, but he had turned away and proved to himself that he was indeed a coward. Igor made up his mind that he would say nothing about what he had witnessed, because his best friend Qren and the rest of the villagers would want to know why he had not tried to save the boy.

Igor finally climbed from his bed and tied on his leather loin cloth, sorted out his brightly coloured beaded hair and pushed his shaped bone through his nose. He picked up the now stone cold boys arm with a piece of cloth, rolled it up and left the farmhouse with his best spear and headed for one of the woodland paths. He had decided to bury the arm and tell no-one about it, that done he turned and made his way to the centre of the village.

That's where he met his best friend Qren whose lithe brown body and various body adornments almost mirrored his own. His friend informed him that the nice family that lived in the end hut nearest the forest had all been killed in the darkness of the previous night, and the youngest son Mika had been carried off into the forest, by the murderous wolf.

His screams for help had been heard by many of the inhabitants, but no- one had gone to his aid. Igor couldn't look Qren in the eyes, as his guilt suddenly got the better of him. He made his excuses and hid himself away in the darkest corner of the barn, where he sat by the side of the big bull Midvant and cried the tears of shame, until he finally fell asleep.

Igor knew that he was not brave enough to protect his mother and sister Jisga should it come to it, because he had actually seen the feared Zolem once before. One day, years ago, when he had been out collecting nuts from the height of a tall tree, he had watched motionless as the huge silver coated wolf stopped under the very tree in which he was hiding. The big beast lifted his black nose and sniffed the air in every direction. Zolem knew that Igor was there. Igor could see the wickedness and cunning in the wolf's white eyes as the villagers searched the dense forest for him. Igor was shaking so much that he almost fell from the top of the tree to land by Zolem's paws. For no apparent reason the beast sat down and lifted his nose into the air, opened his huge mouth slightly to release a long mournful howl. The sad terrifying sound seemed to last forever. Igor was convinced that it was the beast's death cry, and it was meant just for him, and that the killer wolf could somehow feel Igor's body trembling through the roots of the nearby tree.

Igor clung onto the tree trunk for dear life, even though the killer was long gone. Still, he held on so tightly that his arms and legs no longer had any feeling left in them. His eyes continued to search the darkness below for any sign of danger. As the long cold hours of night slowly came and went, the still violently trembling cowardly Igor stayed hidden up at the top of the tree swaying in the wind. The sound of Zolem's howl was still ringing loudly in his ears, a sound that would haunt him forever.

Igor could hear the villagers search party calling his name from below, but he was too cold, stiff and numb to answer them. They continued to call out until they got close to his hiding place. His best friend Qren was the first to see him by pointing his muscular arm excitedly into the top of the tall green leaved tree. Relieved villagers called his name and waved their arms as they tried desperately to encourage him to climb down, but no matter what they said and whoever called out to him, his arms and legs were so petrified with fear, that Igor still clung numbly to the tree trunk.

In the end it was Qren and two other young men who clambered up the tree and helped their friend to climb down. Igor's feet finally touched the hard earth and his eyes immediately darted in every direction in his search for the silver wolf. The huge beast had recently been sitting in the very same spot on which he was now standing. It took his mother, Zirra, many days to get her trembling son to tell of the terror that had affected him so badly.

Chief Axum and the elders listened intently as he told his fearsome tale. They all agreed that something had to be done to stop Zolem. But what? No matter what attempts they had tried in the past, what traps they had set, how many hunting parties had left the village in search of Zolem, the cunning silver wolf always seemed to be one step ahead of them.

CHAPTER 3

The fluffy 'white rain' lay cold and deep on the frozen ground, piled high on the trees and roofs of the mud huts, completely covering the much needed grass that usually fed the animals. Igor opened the thick wooden door of his mother's hut to the sight of a complete covering of white rain. He glanced at the silent eery forest and wondered if the killer was there, watching and just waiting for his chance to attack him. Igor had no choice but to venture outside, it was his duty to check on the animals. After only a few silent steps in the white snow, he stopped dead in his tracks, because when he looked down he could see the unmistakably deep paw prints of the ghostly Zolem. The wolf had circled the farmhouse many times during the night time in his efforts to gain entry.

Cries of anguish filled the early morning air as another villager discovered his animals dead, injured or missing. Igor looked into the fenced off area where his remaining two animals should have been. All that he could see was a dead white goat and a long blood stained trail in the white rain that led off into the depths of the fearsome forest, where one of his poor animals had been taken away never to return. Igor ran over to the barn to find the blood covered Midvant standing cowering in the far corner of the barn. Great flaps of the bull's tough skin were hanging from his bulky brown flanks, revealing raw red blood dripping flesh beneath.

He turned and ran as fast as he could to his mother's hut to tell her what had happened. She quickly pulled her wrap tightly around her shoulders and followed her son back to the barn. Zirra examined the huge, trembling, blood spattered animal. She called out urgent instructions to Igor. He had to fetch the spell master and old mother Binza to tell her to bring her medicine bag. When Igor returned with the wise old women, he was told to go outside and to leave them to their work. He had to wait outside just in case he was needed, while they did what they could for the poor trembling bull.

Igor sat outside the barn for hours as the spell master chanted his magic incantations whilst the massive bull bellowed in pain as the two women did their best to stitch up his awful wounds. Salty tears ran freely down Igor's brown face, because he blamed himself for the loss of his stock. If only he had been there last night. If only his father had made him more brave, then maybe he could have done something, anything.

Even if he had been killed by the beast in a rescue attempt of the boy, at least the villagers would have been proud of him. His mother and Binza the medicine woman finally came out of the barn. His mother thanked her old friend for her help. Igor wanted to go into the barn to see the big bull, but the spell master was still casting his ancient magic, although in the past the old man's rituals had done very little to help in the battle against the threat.

Igor spent the next two days hiding away in the barn with Midvant. He told the great bull all about his cowardice as he tended the animal's seeping wounds. He repeated the treatments every hour as he whispered non-stop in the massive bull's ear. Night time was the worst because he knew that Zolem was out there somewhere, just waiting for him to make a mistake. He also knew that the wolf would be looking for a way to get into the barn again. Igor had been around every inch of the inner walls, over and over again. He was confident that after his repairs to the barn, he and the injured bull were safe, at least for the time being.

Late into the second night the big bull began snorting loudly and pulling on the rope that tethered him to the barn wall. Midvant sensed something. The loud noise woke Igor from a deep sleep. He grabbed his night stick and sat trembling as he calmed the massive bull by talking quietly to him. Igor listened intently until suddenly he heard Zolem snorting and sniffing at the bottom of the barn doors. Igor's eyes and ears followed the growling, sniffing beast as it searched every inch of the outside wall of the building looking for any weakness.
After a while Igor heard no more sound. He was convinced that Zolem had given up and moved on to search somewhere else for his dinner. Igor was falling asleep again when he heard a loud scratching noise coming from the bottom of the barn door, Midvant began snorting and stamping on the hard earth as he got the unmistakable scent of the killer. With trembling hands Igor used his flint to light the oil lamp. Hearing a scraping noise, he walked slowly with stiff legs towards the locked door.

When he looked down he could see the huge silver front paws of the wolf as the killer tried to dig a tunnel under the door. Igor could smell the beast's pungent pong. He could hear the beast snarling and growling in its efforts to get in. Igor began banging on the door and shouting as loud as he could, but that only told Zolem that he was inside. That knowledge alone seemed to make the wolf dig even faster. Igor looked around the cold dark barn that was filled with tools that they used to work the land. He needed to find a weapon with which to fight the wolf should he get in.

His eyes locked onto a hay pitchfork which had two very sharp pointed tines. He grabbed the long wooden fork in both hands and rushed back to the big wooden door and began stabbing at the massive paws as they scratched away at the cold hard earth. Igor had not realised it but in his terrified state he was now screaming as loud as he could. Igor stabbed over and over at the massive paws. He could hear Zolem growling and snorting as he increased his effort to gain entry. The killer's only intention was to kill Igor or the bull. He would then eat his fill of whichever one he chose.

All of a sudden, a loud high pitched yelp of pain came from the other side of the barn door. No longer were there huge menacing looking paws with long white claws scratching at the cold earth, and there was no longer any sound to be heard from the wolf. Igor suddenly stopped stabbing and with a heaving chest, placed his ear against the wooden door and listened intently.

The only sound that he could hear was the howl of the cold wind and the distant whimpering of the injured wolf as it slowly limped away. Igor looked down at the dark red blood dripping from the tine of the hay fork and smiled to himself, because now he knew that the beast could be beaten.

Zolem was no longer invincible. If only Igor was clever enough, brave enough to figure out a way to kill Zolem, it would make the village safe again and they could all return to a normal tranquil life, the same as it was before the terror of Zolem was thrust upon them.

CHAPTER 4

Igor had proudly shown the bloodied tine of the hay fork to his best friend Qren and told him of how he desperately tried to protect himself and his grandfather when the beast, Zolem, had tried to dig his way into the barn. He had even shown Qren the trail of the wolf's red blood spots, as they zig-zagged off into the deep dark forest. Qren embellished the tale of Igor's fight with Zolem, and every time he told the story it meant that Igor's skirmish with the wolf soon became a hand to hand combat with the beast. As the story spread around the village, Igor instantly became the village hero. Chief Axum lived there with his wives and three beautiful teenage daughters in the only stone house that had been built in the village.

When he heard about Igor's fight with Zolem he immediately summoned Igor to his house. Igor was shown into the chief's chambers where the leader of the village sat proudly on a huge throne-like wooden chair. In his right hand he held a long spear with a gold pointed barbed head. Behind him, mounted on the stone wall were the white skeletal heads of the many animals that he had supposedly killed. The chief himself wore his ceremonial head dress which was made out of long brightly coloured tail feathers, all collected from many of the dark forest's birds. All of them were held in place by a red leather head band to make the feathers stand upright.

Through his broad nose, Axum had a large ceremonial golden bone and around his neck, upper arms and just below the knees there were tied the white teeth of many different sizes. According to legend they were all from the alligator that in his youth the king had supposedly killed, using only his bare hands. Igor knelt in front of the chief until he was told to stand. The younger man looked nervously into the pale eyes of the potbellied chief. Axum's main wife and their three daughters all gazed at him in admiration, because they had heard the story of his titanic battle with Zolem.

But the brave brown skinned young man only had eyes for the beauty of the chief's second eldest daughter, who, like her sisters, had long beaded hair that hung down to her waist and also thick gold chains that hung loosely around her beautiful thin neck. Her nose bone was also made of gold. She blushed crimson under his gaze and eventually smiled at him before she nervously turned away. The chief coughed loudly forcing Igor to return his gaze back to the old man, who stared at him for a long time before saying in a very high-pitched voice that sounded like a squealing piglet.

18

"So young man, I understand that you alone have battled the beast Zolem and driven him away from our village. For that you will be rewarded with five goats and two cows from my very own herd. Now, Igor, I have an offer for you and only you.

If you can kill this beast, Zolem, and bring his body to me, I will build you a house just like this one and you can choose any one of my beautiful daughters, to marry and share the house with. You have until the moon is full again to complete your quest.

Now, go and bring me the body of Zolem".

With a quick final glance at the beautiful second daughter, who again blushed a deep scarlet, he left the chief's house and went in search of Qren.

CHAPTER 5

Igor dragged Qren into the quiet of the barn and told him what the chief had said. He begged his best friend to help him kill Zolem, but Qren wanted nothing to do with it and left his best friend sitting in the barn, disappointed, alone and deep in thought. Igor knew that he was not brave enough to kill the beast all on his own; he would need help but who would help him? Who could he ask? His grandfather was too old; his sisters were all too young and too busy beading everyone's hair. He couldn't ask his mother. That left only himself. If only his father was still there, he would know exactly what to do.

Igor sat on his own in the dusty barn thinking for hours. Eventually he slipped into a deep sleep, but his vivid dreams were entirely filled with the chief's second daughter. Would his love for her perhaps give him the added courage that he needed, for when he finally faced the wolf devil? Her bright blue eyes were the most beautiful eyes he had ever seen. He just had to find a way to kill Zolem and with that thought still in his head, he eventually drifted into a deep, coma like sleep.

Out of the dusty beams of the barn a miracle seemed to happen. A vision of his dead father appeared to him and said to him,

"Look up into the roof of the barn my son and be brave".

He suddenly woke, jumped up, and shook his head. He looked around the empty barn for his father, but he wasn't there. He sat back down and thought about what the vision had just said to him. He looked up into the roof of the dusty old barn and all that he could see was the large sacks of grain and nuts that were hanging high in the rafters. This had been done to protect the much needed food supply from the rats and mice. The sacks were held in place by thick ropes that were hung over rafters and tied at the side of the barn with large metal hooks.

When the sacks were needed, two or three big strong men would undo the ropes and lower the heavy sacks down to the ground. Igor had seen such a sack that fell from the rafters many years ago when his father had been alive and it had exploded, spreading corn into every corner of the barn. It had taken him days to clear the up mess.

For days Igor had been sitting and staring at the heavy sacks in the roof of the barn. He knew that his father was trying to tell him the answer to his quest, but he couldn't see what use a sack of corn could be against the powerful man-eating beast. Maybe if he went to sleep again, his father would show him exactly what he meant and solve the riddle. So Igor slept the sleep of the dead, but still his father didn't reappear.

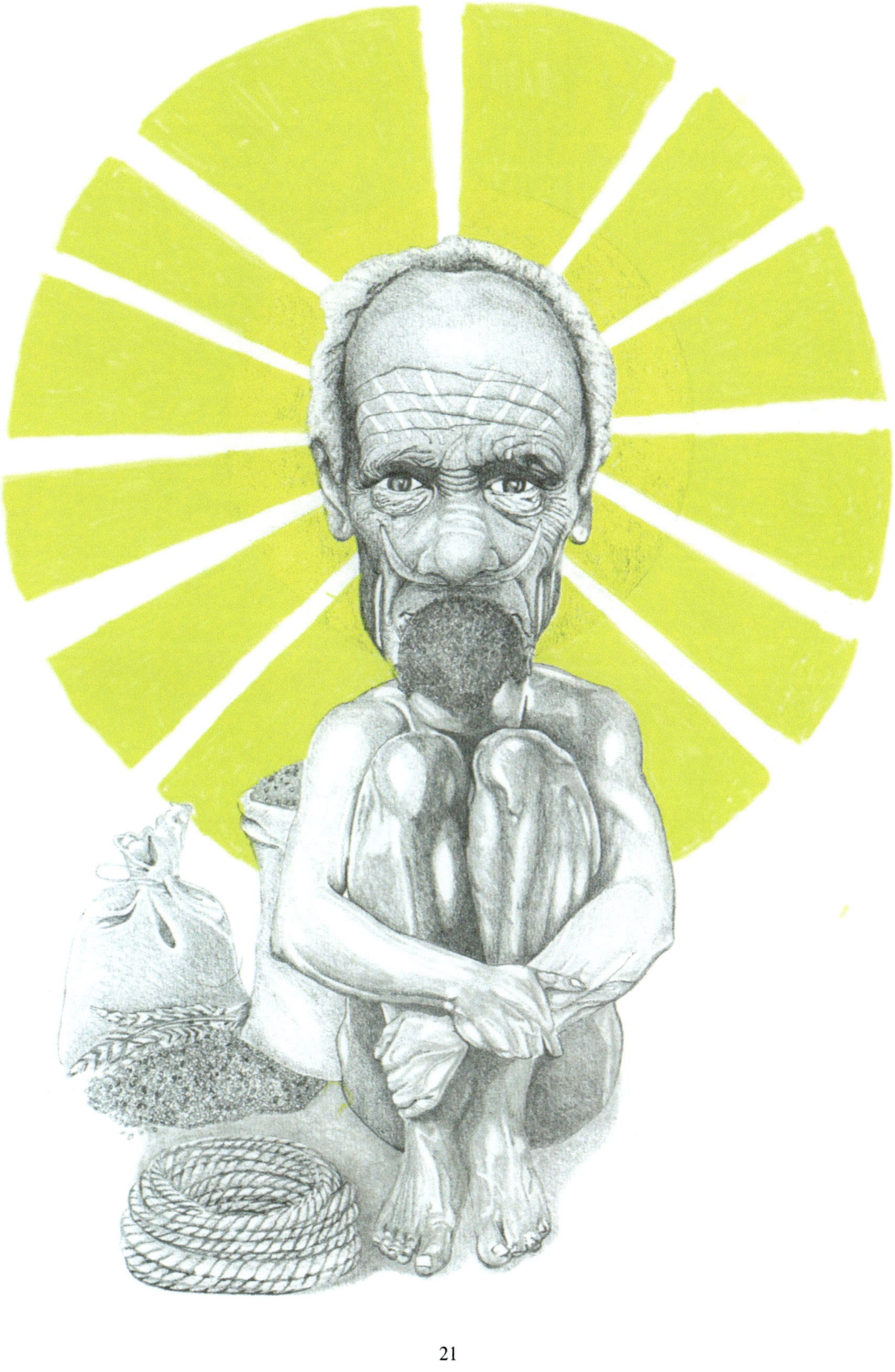

Fast running out of time he began to think that he had failed in his quest before it had even begun. When, on the third day, as he slept in the afternoon, his father's vision reappeared and said,

"Now, look at the way that it works, and be brave my son".

Igor woke with a start and studied the heavy sacks for the hundredth time. Only now did his eyes follow the ropes that ran from the necks of the hanging sacks all the way down to where each one of the sacks is tethered at the side of the barn, and it was only then that he could finally see what his father was trying to tell him. He smiled to himself and began planning the best way to set his trap, because at last, he now knew how he would kill the wolf, that will allow him to claim his prize.

Igor finally had everything worked out in his mind. He now had a plan of how he would trap and kill the beast. The only problem being, was he brave enough to make his plan work? He took a slow walk around the edge of the forest in the daylight and finally found the exact tree that would best suit his needs. Having found it he stood looking up into the tree's highest branches, selecting in his mind the one which he thought was the perfect bough for his plan.

He climbed the chosen tree and sat on a wide bough and looked down at the white earth far below. He then pictured in his mind, just how his plan would work. He would need the help of at least three strong men, a large sack of rocks, a long rope, a very sharp knife and the bravery of a hundred men.

CHAPTER 6

The old oak tree that he had chosen had a large fork in its trunk that Igor would fit into quite nicely. The next day he stood inside the recess and realised that if his plan failed, it would be his last day on earth, and he would be Zolem's dinner. Igor climbed up to the tree top and sat on the bough that would best suit his needs.

He straddled the thick branch and cut a round groove in the thick black bark, checking that it was directly above the recess of the tree. Pleased with his work, he climbed back down and walked back to the village in search of a strong rope that was long enough to go over the thick bough, and then reach to the ground on the other side.

With the help of Qren he carried a large amount of rocks to the base of the tree. When he thought that he had enough rocks to serve his purpose, he walked back to the barn and selected a large heavy corn sack that would be suitable for his needs. Back at the old oak tree he filled the sack with the rocks and when the sack was almost full, he used all of his might as he tied a knot in the neck of the sack, so that that would allow him to then tie the thick rope around the underside of the knot. With this part of his trap complete, he began work on the next stage of his plan. He dug around a thick tree root that was jutting half out of the frozen ground, precisely where he wanted it to be. He made a hole big enough under the root so that he could tie a thinner piece of rope around the exposed root.

Once that job was done, he cut a man sized piece of the thinner rope, which he would need for the next stage of his plan. Igor used a long length of thin string to measure the exact position in the stronger rope, that is where he will need to place another knot. When he was certain that he had the correct place, he tied a slip knot into the rope. He then measured a man's height down from the knot and formed a large loop in the thicker rope. With everything now in place, all he required now was the help of three strong men.

The strongest men from the village heaved the heavy sack full of rocks high up into the tree top. They held the rope still while Igor tied the thinner rope around the big knot that he had already tied in the thick rope. That done the men gradually let the weight of the sack sink down until all the weight of the rocks was being supported by the much thinner rope, which was tightly tied around the root of the tree. He then tied a large slip knot in the remaining thick rope that he had laid out in a circle in the dip in front of the tree, he then covered the rope with some of the fresh white snow. With his plan now complete, he stood in front of the oak tree and prayed to the Sun God that he had done his calculations correctly, and that his plan would work.

His trap was finally ready and in place. He stood back and admired his handy work one last time. All he needed then was the bravery of a hundred men to fulfil his dream, but when he visualised the beauty of the chief's second daughter; the sight of the young boy being taken away by the wolf; and with his father watching over him, he now knew that live or die, he was finally brave enough and ready to go through with his plan to kill Zolem.

Igor spent some spiritual time with his mother and sisters who painted his face and upper body as if he was going into battle. Binza, his mother, presented her brave son with his father's favourite spear, which he had accidentally left behind the last time that he had walked into the dark forest.

Igor's mother had sent for the spell master to cast a spell of bravery over Igor before he walked into the forest, just as his father had done, all that time ago. Igor walked bravely towards the track that led to the brown water at the edge of the forest, he stopped, turned and waved goodbye to his family. He proudly held his father's spear in the air as if in final salute, before he turned and headed towards the old oak tree, and what might be certain death.

When he arrived at the trap site, he covered his tracks by ruffling the cold snow with the tip of the spear. He looked up into the grey sky, and said a silent prayer to the Sun God one last time before he took up his position inside the recess of the tree and began his wait for Zolem. He heard the voice of his father, and believed that the spirit of his father was again telling him to be brave. Igor stood with the sharp knife in his right hand and waited patiently for the wolf to appear.

Igor finally heard the wolf's raspy breathing before the killer actually came into view. He could hear the beast growling under its breath as it walked slowly towards the village. Suddenly the wolf came to a sudden stop. Zolem lifted his black nose and took a long, noisy sniff of the air.

Igor was trembling from head to toe. He wanted to run but knew in his heart that that would be a big mistake and certain death, so he slowly moved his trembling hand that held the knife towards the thin rope. Igor held his breath. He could now smell the beast, as the wolf's black twitching nose came into view, followed by the long white snout and then the white evil looking unblinking eyes. The beast had its ears laid flat against his head as he stared at Igor. Igor stood motionless as the huge beast lowered its wide head to sniff the air around the base of the old oak tree.

Zolem inched slowly forward, his eyes narrowed. He stood motionless staring at Igor. The beast began growling as he curled his lips at the side of his mouth, and bared his long sharp white teeth. The silver beast stood still and looked nervously at Igor with his war paint on. Instinctively, somehow Zolem knew that it was a trap. Growling, he took a tentative half step towards Igor, his left paw landing just inside the hidden circle of rope.

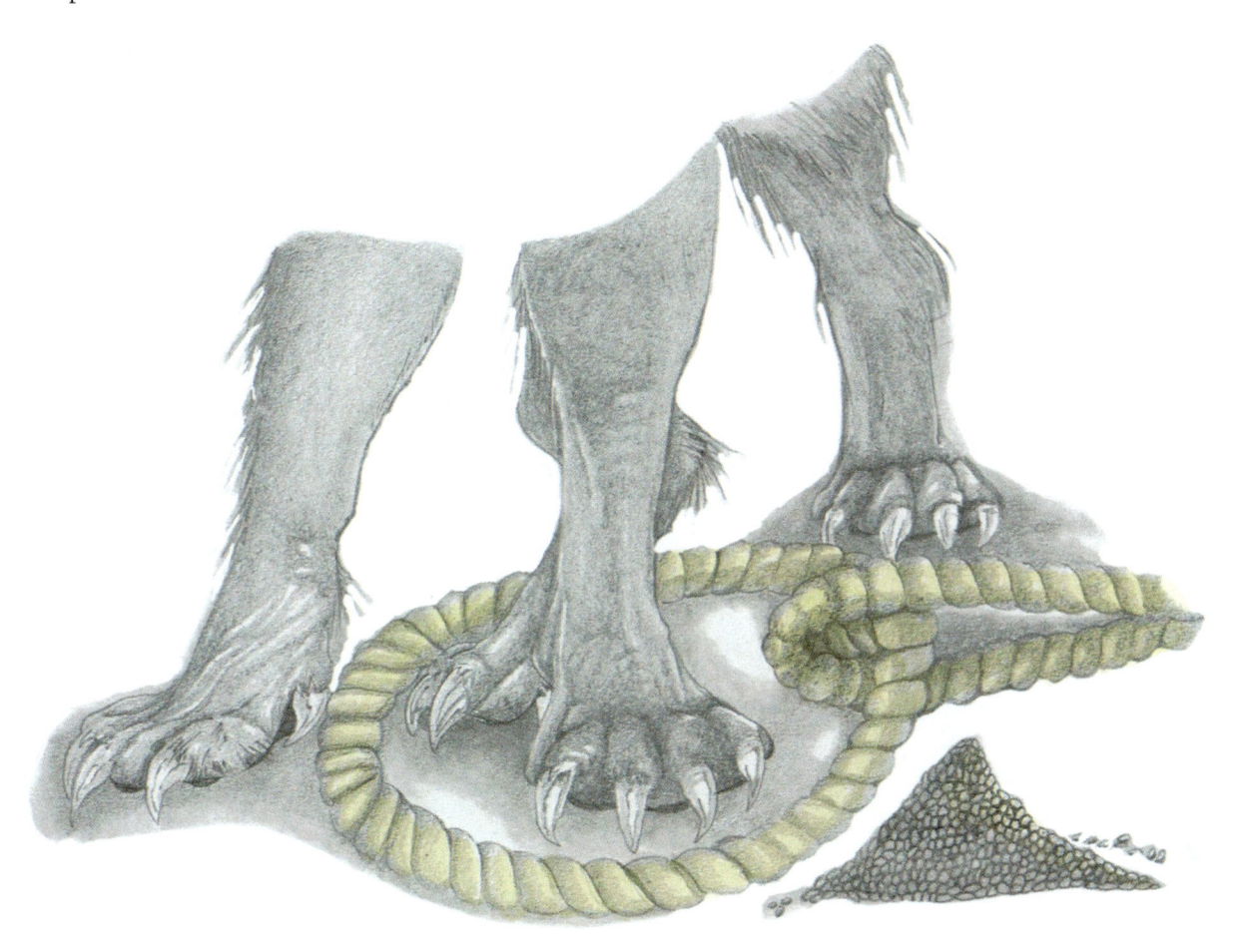

Igor could smell the animal's foul breath and pungent pong. He watched closely and with all his heart, he willed the monster to take just one more step. But the wolf just stood perfectly still and with its chilling unblinking white eyes he stared at Igor. They stared at each other, eyeball to eyeball, one trembling with fear because he could smell the foul breath of the wolf and his odour, the other growling, growing in confidence with dribblets of white drool dropping from its sharp teeth.

The cunning wolf clearly wondered at the unfamiliar behaviour of a man standing inside an old, almost dead tree? It didn't seem right somehow.

Neither moved as they continued to stare at one another. Zolem's growl seemed to come from somewhere deep within his huge body. Igor was the first to lose his nerve. He began shouting at the wolf.

"Come on you devil, take another step, just one last step and I will have you."

Zolem remained where he was and continued to stare menacingly at Igor, frothy drool now dripping from both sides of its huge mouth. The wolf, ready to pounce, moved ever so slowly towards a now confident Igor who rested the razor sharp blade against the thin rope. He held his breath as the wolf lifted its other front paw, but stopped himself mid stride. Again he held himself dead still, his eyes suddenly suspicious at Igor's strange defiant behaviour. Igor continued to shout. Zolem snarled and growled back at him, searching Igor's face with blood lust in its chilling white eyes.

Igor kicked out at the wolf with his right foot. The beast snapped at it with his gleaming white teeth. Igor kicked out again and this time the ever confident wolf took his final step. At last, the wolf was standing inside the circle of rope, exactly where Igor wanted him.

"NOW"

Igor shouted to himself, drawing the sharp knife across the thin rope. The sack of rocks, high in the tree, is suddenly released and crashed against the cold earth with a thud. Within a heartbeat, the wolf yelped out aloud in terror as the rope tightened around his front legs and he was lifted bodily from the ground and was dragged snarling and yelping up into the air, trapped by the lasso around his body, the rope sinking into the killers soft flesh ever tightening its grip around Zolem's front legs as he struggled to get free. The wolf thrashed about for all it was worth as it tried its best to escape, its long legs and body jerking in all possible directions, as it fought against its bonds.

Igor grabbed his father's spear and began to climb the tree to where Zolem was howling and thrashing around.

Igor drew level with the huge beast, who stopped thrashing through exhaustion and just hung limply in the air as it watched Igor. The trussed-up wolf was helpless suspended in midair, its hateful white eyes locked onto Igor as it gently spun in the wind. Igor sat on a branch level with the mighty wolf. He drew back his right arm and using all his strength, he drove the sharp tip of his father's spear as far as he could into the wolf's tough body.

The wolf cried out at in agony as the sharp pointed spear passed right through him over and over until Zolem finally hung there lifeless, red blood oozing out of every wound. The wolf's wild white eyes rolled back in its huge head which was hanging to one side, its thick black tongue hanging from the side of its still gaping mouth.

Igor didn't stop stabbing the wolf until he finally ran out of breath, exhausted. He left his father's spear buried deep in the wolf's body and protruding out of the top of the blood covered animals head. He sat back and leaned against the trunk of the tree and caught his breath. He looked at the killer's blood that oozed from the various holes in the beast's lifeless body.

Igor watched as the thick red blood, some of it congealed, the rest dripping from the tip of the dead wolfs magnificently thick tail. He sat not moving on the branch until the sun came up the next morning. He finally climbed down from the tree and walked through the cold, knee deep snow that lay on the ground, back into the village. He walked to the centre of the village, fell to his knees shouting.

"The wolf is dead, Zolem is dead, I have killed the beast".

Villagers slowly emerged from their warm huts and looked at the young man who knelt in the cold snow telling them over and over that the beast, Zolem, was dead. People just stood and stared at him disbelievingly, acting as if he was mad. Finally, the chief walked up to him, who was at last being congratulated, and given thanks by anyone that was close enough to him to do so. The chief held out his weathered hand in the air and silenced the excitable onlookers.

He looked at Igor who said,

"Zolem is dead, I have killed the beast".

More and more people began to come out of their huts, slowly at first, and then as the excitement grew everyone began cheering.

The excited villagers became silent when the chief asked the young man

"Where is the body of Zolem, show me the body of the beast, prove to me that the beast is dead".

Igor led the way to the old oak tree, the disbelieving chief following close behind leading a procession of silent villagers. Igor stopped beneath the slowly turning body, pointing up into the branches at the dead wolf. No one dared to speak. Everyone just stared at the *massive creature that had terrorised them for so long. The chief demanded that the wolf be cut down and its hide removed where it lay.

"I want the beasts hide dried and then presented to my second daughter on her wedding day, the day that she is to be married to our hero, Igor".

Every villager clapped their hands and cheered as they carried Igor back to the village, where his proud mother and sisters waited to congratulate him.

CHAPTER 7

As a proud father the chief kept his promise and had a house built out of stone as a wedding present for his second daughter, Zafira, who happily took the hand of her husband, Igor. Now they were man and wife resting in front of a roaring fire, laying together on the silver rug that was made out of Zolem's fur.

The happy couple would never want for anything throughout their lives, because Igor was the saviour of the village, a man of legend, a man of property and in due course, the father of many children.

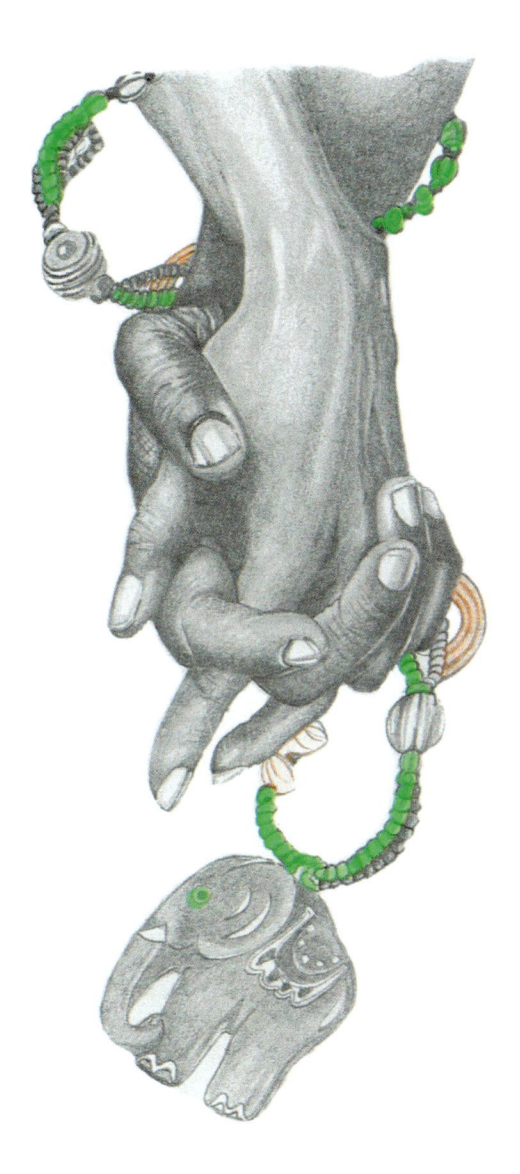

Igor, now an old man is the village story teller and no matter which story he tells to his listeners, the demise of Zolem is always the most requested story.

The End

ABOUT THE AUTHOR

Brian is a new author, he is a long-term dialysis patient of over 20 years and uses his 4 weekly sessions of treatment to write his many different genres of books, these include fiction novels, a biography [A Badsey Boy] and many beautifully illustrated children's books.

Born in the mid 50s, Brian is a disabled man with a lifelong passion for angling, when his illness forced his retirement, he discovered his creative imagination, which shows in his love of writing.

Printed in Poland
by Amazon Fulfillment
Poland Sp. z o.o., Wrocław